MYSTERIES & MARVELS OF THE ANIMAL WORLD

Karen Goaman and Heather Amery

Consultant: Joyce Pope

Designed by Anne Sharples
and Nigel Frey

Illustrated by David Quinn
Sarah DeAth (Linden Artists), Ian Jackson,
Rob McCaig, Chris Shields (Wilcock Riley),
and David Wright (Jillian Burgess)

Cartoons by John Shackell

First published in 1983
by Usborne Publishing Ltd, 20 Garrick Street,
London WC2E 9BJ.
© 1983 by Usborne Publishing Ltd.

The name Usborne and the device are Trade Marks
of Usborne Publishing Ltd.

Printed in Great Britain by
Blantyre Printing and Binding Ltd, London and Glasgow.

The Fennec Fox lives in hot deserts.

A Lioness carries her cub to a new resting place.

Contents

The Spiny Anteater, lays eggs.

A Gorilla uses a large leaf as an umbrella.

A Grizzly Bear lives on a wide variety of food.

The Aardvaark is almost naked.

The Duck-billed Platypus feeds underwater but breathes air.

About this book

This book is a fascinating introduction to the world of land mammals. By concentrating on the unusual, the extraordinary and the unexplained, it provides a stimulating starting point to a study of many aspects of mammal life, such as the way they live in different habitats, find food, move about and communicate.

Mammals are different from other land animals, such as birds, insects, snakes or frogs, although they do have some things in common. All mammals breathe air and are warm-blooded and most have fur or hair. Mammals give birth to live young (except two which lay eggs) and all females produce milk for their babies and care for them. Many mammals are intelligent and curious, using tools, trying new foods and exploring new environments.

This book will lead to an understanding of the huge variety and interdependence of mammal life but points out that there is still much to be discovered about mammals and the way they live in the wild.

A Giant Panda mainly eats bamboo.

TRUE or FALSE?

Look out for these questions and try to guess if they are true or false. The answers are on p. 32.

A Kongoni calf feeding on its mother's milk.

Strange start to life

Most mammals give birth to babies which are fully formed. But two strange mammals lay eggs and the young of marsupials, such as the Kangaroos, develop in their mothers' pouches.

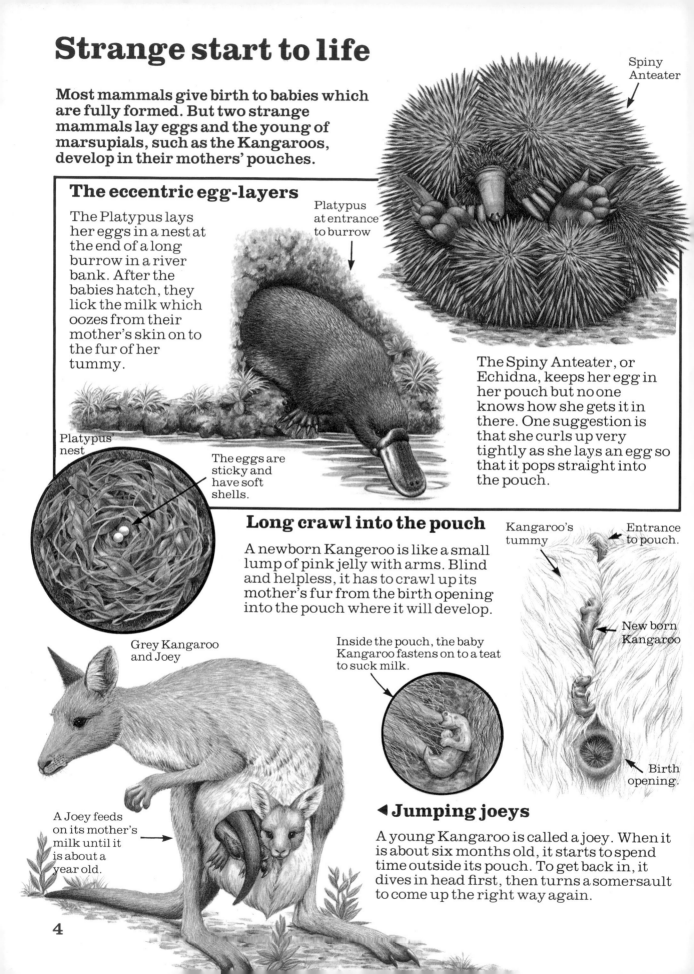

Spiny Anteater

The eccentric egg-layers

The Platypus lays her eggs in a nest at the end of a long burrow in a river bank. After the babies hatch, they lick the milk which oozes from their mother's skin on to the fur of her tummy.

Platypus at entrance to burrow

The Spiny Anteater, or Echidna, keeps her egg in her pouch but no one knows how she gets it in there. One suggestion is that she curls up very tightly as she lays an egg so that it pops straight into the pouch.

Platypus nest

The eggs are sticky and have soft shells.

Long crawl into the pouch

A newborn Kangeroo is like a small lump of pink jelly with arms. Blind and helpless, it has to crawl up its mother's fur from the birth opening into the pouch where it will develop.

Kangaroo's tummy

Entrance to pouch.

New born Kangaroo

Birth opening.

Grey Kangaroo and Joey

Inside the pouch, the baby Kangaroo fastens on to a teat to suck milk.

A Joey feeds on its mother's milk until it is about a year old.

◄ Jumping joeys

A young Kangaroo is called a joey. When it is about six months old, it starts to spend time outside its pouch. To get back in, it dives in head first, then turns a somersault to come up the right way again.

4

Growing up

Back packers ▶

A Koala baby spends its first six months in its mother's pouch and another six months riding around on her back.

Opossum
with young

The Opossum feeds at night, climbing trees with hands and feet and clinging on with its claws.

The young koala feeds on eucalyptus leaves over its mother's shoulder.

Koala with baby

Clinging on all over ▶

The female Opossum has a big pouch for her eighteen or so babies. But after about ten weeks they grow too big to fit in it. Then she carries them about and they cling on anywhere they can — on her back, tummy and even on her tail.

When a Hippo mother goes off to feed, she finds a baby sitter.

TRUE or FALSE?

Trailing along behind ▼

When a Shrew mother goes out for food, she takes her young with her in a long line, each holding on firmly to the one in front.

White-toothed shrews

Fantastic feeders

Some mammals have some fantastic ways of getting at food and of storing it.

Mole's worm larder ▶

The Mole hunts for earthworms and insects in its tunnels. If it finds more than it can eat, it bites them in the back. This prevents the worms from wriggling away but keeps them alive and fresh for future meals. The Mole then stores the worms in an underground larder, which may contain hundreds of worms. Moles can eat their own weight in worms each day, finding them with a keen sense of smell and a sensitive nose.

Mole with store of worms.

Toothless wonder

The Giant Anteater has no teeth. It tears open ant hills and termites' nests with its long curved claws. Then it pokes in its tongue – 60 cm long – to pick up the insects. These are crushed by the strong walls of its stomach. A Giant Anteater will swallow several thousand ants or termites for a single meal.

Leopards are good climbers and can drag heavy weights up trees.

Spends much of the day resting in trees and hunts at night.

Leopard's tree larder

A Leopard often stores its prey in a tree larder. It will drag an animal it has killed up a tree and lodge it in a forked branch. Here it is safe from scavengers and the leopard has a ready meal when hungry.

Gazelle lodged in the fork of a tree.

Leopard

Aye-Aye

Fantastic finger ▲

The Aye-Aye has an amazingly long and very useful middle finger. It knocks on the dead wood of a tree, listens for insects inside and pulls them out with its finger.

Giant Anteater

The Anteater can collect 500 ants with one lick!

Giraffe tongue ▶

The Giraffe uses its immensely long tongue and strong upper hairy lip to pull leaves off branches.

A giraffe has an extra-large heart to pump blood up its neck to its head.

45 cm long black tongue.

TRUE or FALSE?

Goats in Tunisia jump on donkeys' backs to reach leaves on high branches of trees.

Salt miners ▶

Elephants living on Mount Elgon in Kenya walk into deep caves at night to mine salt. In total darkness, they strike the salty rock with their tusks, pick off lumps with their trunks and grind the rock up in their mouths. They need the salt as part of their diet. The caves have probably been carved out by elephants mining the rock over thousands of years.

Sniffs at rock to see how salty it is.

Strikes rock with tusks.

Supermovers

Swinging through the trees ▶

The Gibbon can hurl itself at top speed through the forest, swinging from tree to tree. It quickly grasps branches with alternate hands, hurling itself on again with each grasp. Moving like this, it can swing across spaces of 15 metres. Its long arms are its main way of getting about in the treetops.

A tail-less ape, a Gibbon can move through the trees faster than a man can run on the ground underneath.

Has a top speed of 16 kph through the trees.

Extremely long arms and very mobile wrists and shoulders.

Sugar Glider feeding on buds and flowers.

Outstretched skin in flight.

Fold of skin.

TRUE or FALSE?

The Gibbon is a tightrope artist.

Red Kangaroo

Gliding parachutist

The Sugar Glider can glide downwards for about 45 metres between trees. It takes a leap and stretches out the flaps of skin between its front and back legs like a parachute. Landing with great accuracy, it quickly climbs up the tree for another leap.

Leaps and bounds ▶

The Red Kangaroo can jump over obstacles as high as 3 metres. Using its very powerful hind legs, it can travel as far as 9 metres in one huge bound. It holds up its thick tail to help it balance when travelling fast. Over short distances, it can reach a speed of about 55 kilometres an hour.

A Cheetah is the fastest land animal.

Flexible spine moves up and down.

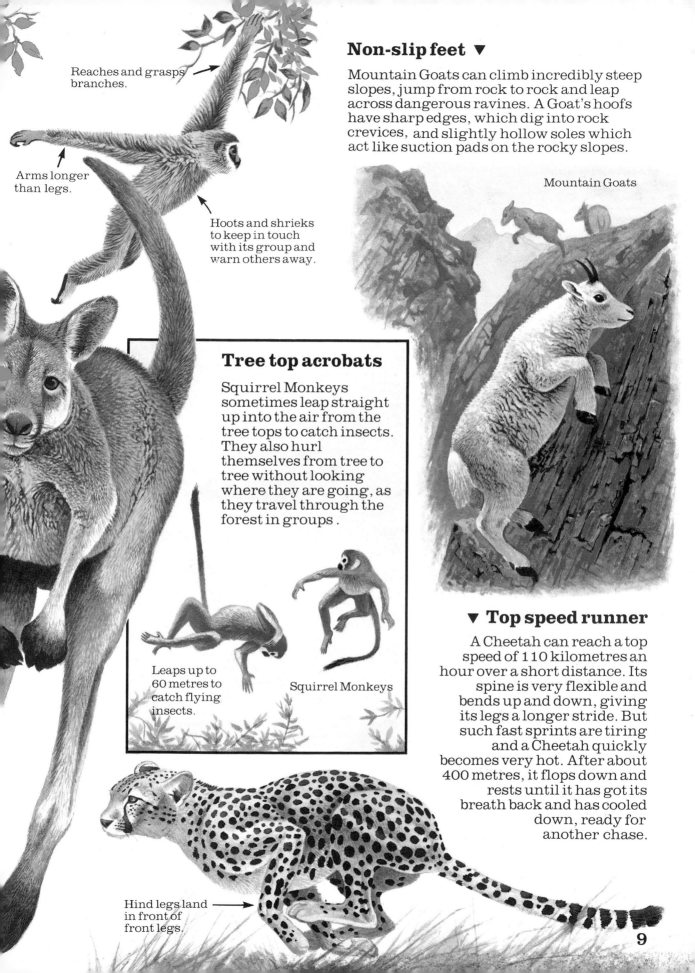

Reaches and grasps branches.

Arms longer than legs.

Hoots and shrieks to keep in touch with its group and warn others away.

Non-slip feet ▼

Mountain Goats can climb incredibly steep slopes, jump from rock to rock and leap across dangerous ravines. A Goat's hoofs have sharp edges, which dig into rock crevices, and slightly hollow soles which act like suction pads on the rocky slopes.

Mountain Goats

Tree top acrobats

Squirrel Monkeys sometimes leap straight up into the air from the tree tops to catch insects. They also hurl themselves from tree to tree without looking where they are going, as they travel through the forest in groups.

Leaps up to 60 metres to catch flying insects.

Squirrel Monkeys

▼ Top speed runner

A Cheetah can reach a top speed of 110 kilometres an hour over a short distance. Its spine is very flexible and bends up and down, giving its legs a longer stride. But such fast sprints are tiring and a Cheetah quickly becomes very hot. After about 400 metres, it flops down and rests until it has got its breath back and has cooled down, ready for another chase.

Hind legs land in front of front legs.

Midnight feasts

Some mammals sleep during the day, waking up at dusk for a busy night.

Blood-sucking vampires ▶

Vampire bats drink the blood of sleeping victims. During the night, they settle on a large animal, such as a cow. They make a very shallow bite which does not wake up the animal. Then they lap up the blood which runs from the wound. Their saliva contains a substance which prevents the blood from clotting and closing up the wound.

The black "devil"

How did the Tasmanian Devil get its name? Because it has a devilish snarl and a gaping mouth with strong teeth. It hunts at night, ambushing its prey which it pushes into its mouth with its front feet. But it looks more like a small, stubby bear than a devil.

Its heavy jaws can open to nearly a right angle.

Eats any flesh, alive or dead.

Tasmanian Devil

The laughing hyaenas ▶

Hyaenas set out at night to hunt in packs of up to 30. They run down a large animal, such as a wildebeest, biting it with their powerful jaws until it falls. After about 15 minutes, they have eaten every scrap, even cracking up bones with their strong teeth, and leaving no trace of the night's meal.

Uses ears and nose more than eyes to find its prey.

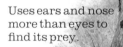

Spotted Haenas

Frog-eating Bats choose the juiciest frog by listening to its mating call.

Daytime earplugs ▼

The Bushbaby has amazingly sharp hearing to help it find food in the dark. Its hearing is so good that when it sleeps during the day, it has to fold its ears inwards to plug up its earholes. Otherwise all the noises of the forest would keep it awake all day. It takes great care of its ears, curling them up before it leaps so that they do not catch on branches.

It can turn its head right round to look directly behind it.

Tarsier

Bushbaby

It can make huge leaps — up to 6 metres — from tree to tree.

The Bushbaby gets its name from the cries it makes at night which sound like a new-born baby.

The hyaena's call is a sad howl but when excited it gives a mad cackle.

Huge eyes ▲

The Tarsier's enormous eyes help it to see in the dark. It leaps like a frog, with jumps up to 2 metres, through the forest at night, searching for insects, young birds, eggs and lizards to eat. It has sticky round toe pads to help it cling to branches.

Curious and confusing colours

The changing colours

The Arctic Fox is smoky grey or brown in summer but in winter it turns white, making it hard to see against a background of snow and ice.

As the days get longer, it loses its white fur and grows grey fur. As the days shorten, white fur grows back again.

Summer coat

Under the coarse outer fur is a thick woolly layer which protects it from the Arctic cold.

Winter coat

Golden Lion Marmoset

Confusing stripes ▼

A Zebra's stripes may seem to make it very easily seen but, in the heat haze of the African plains, the stripes blur its outline. They act as a camouflage, especially when it is moving, and confuse its predators.

TRUE or FALSE?

Black Panthers really do exist in the forests of South America.

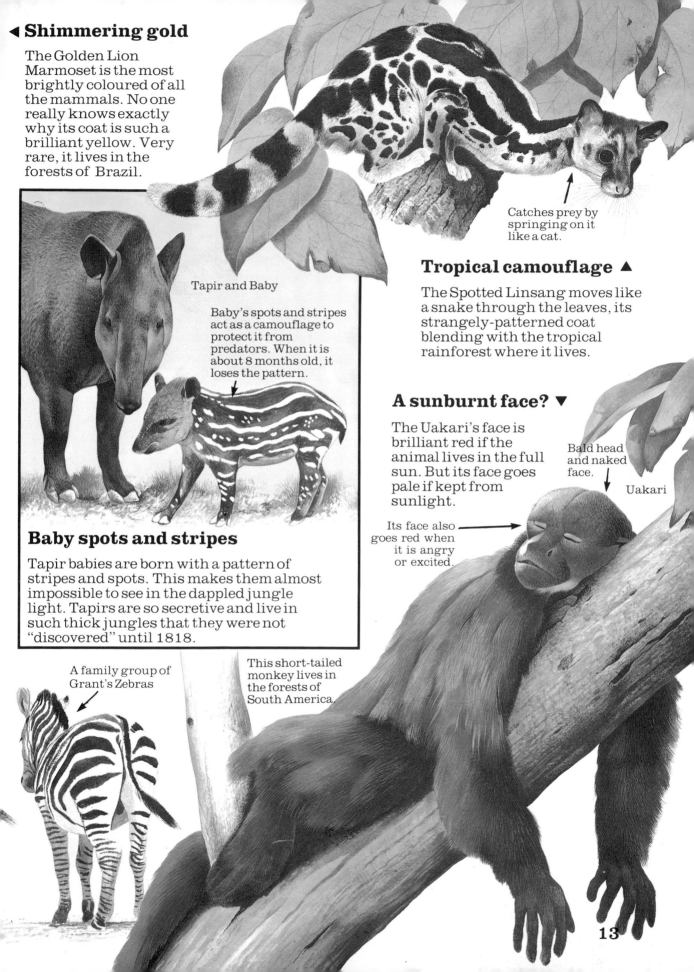

◄ Shimmering gold

The Golden Lion Marmoset is the most brightly coloured of all the mammals. No one really knows exactly why its coat is such a brilliant yellow. Very rare, it lives in the forests of Brazil.

Catches prey by springing on it like a cat.

Tropical camouflage ▲

The Spotted Linsang moves like a snake through the leaves, its strangely-patterned coat blending with the tropical rainforest where it lives.

Tapir and Baby

Baby's spots and stripes act as a camouflage to protect it from predators. When it is about 8 months old, it loses the pattern.

A sunburnt face? ▼

The Uakari's face is brilliant red if the animal lives in the full sun. But its face goes pale if kept from sunlight.

Bald head and naked face.

Uakari

Its face also goes red when it is angry or excited.

Baby spots and stripes

Tapir babies are born with a pattern of stripes and spots. This makes them almost impossible to see in the dappled jungle light. Tapirs are so secretive and live in such thick jungles that they were not "discovered" until 1818.

A family group of Grant's Zebras

This short-tailed monkey lives in the forests of South America.

13

Escape artists

A Springbok jumping or "pronking".

Springs and bounces ▶

When surprised or alarmed, the Springbok jumps straight up in the air, as high as 3 metres, with its body arched and legs stiff. This sets the whole herd springing and bouncing. No one knows why they do this. It may be a way of warning the herd of danger or it may confuse a predator, such as a cheetah, when it attacks the Springboks.

Springs up, arching back and lowering head.

TRUE or FALSE?

A porcupine shoots its quills at an enemy.

The Spotted Skunk does a handstand to squirt smelly liquid at an enemy.

In spite of their smell, Skunks are sometimes killed by golden eagles, foxes and coyotes.

◀ The smelly squirters

The Skunk, when disturbed, raises it tail, stamps its feet, growls and hisses. If this does not make an enemy retreat, it squirts a horrible-smelling liquid from glands under its tail. Its aim is very accurate with a range of up to 3 metres. The foul scent can be smelt half a kilometre away.

The Striped Skunk turns its back on its enemy to squirt at it.

Playing dead ▶

The Large American Opossum fools its enemies by looking as if it is dead. When attacked, it rolls over and lies still, with open mouth and glassy eyes. A predator may then lose interest and go away. No one knows if the Opossum is pretending to be dead or if it is so scared it is paralysed with fear. But it soon takes a quick look round and, if the danger is over, comes back to life.

Opossum

Heads you win tails you lose

If a Wood Mouse is caught by its tail, it can quickly shed the end part of it, to the surprise of its attacker. But the tail may never grow again.

Suits of armour ▼

Armadillos are protected by hard shells, like suits of armour. The shells are made of plates of bone, covered with scales and linked by leathery skin. This flexible armour extends over the head and down the tail.

The Three-banded Armadillo can roll into a tight ball — no enemy could easily get at this ball of armour.

Nine-banded Armadillo

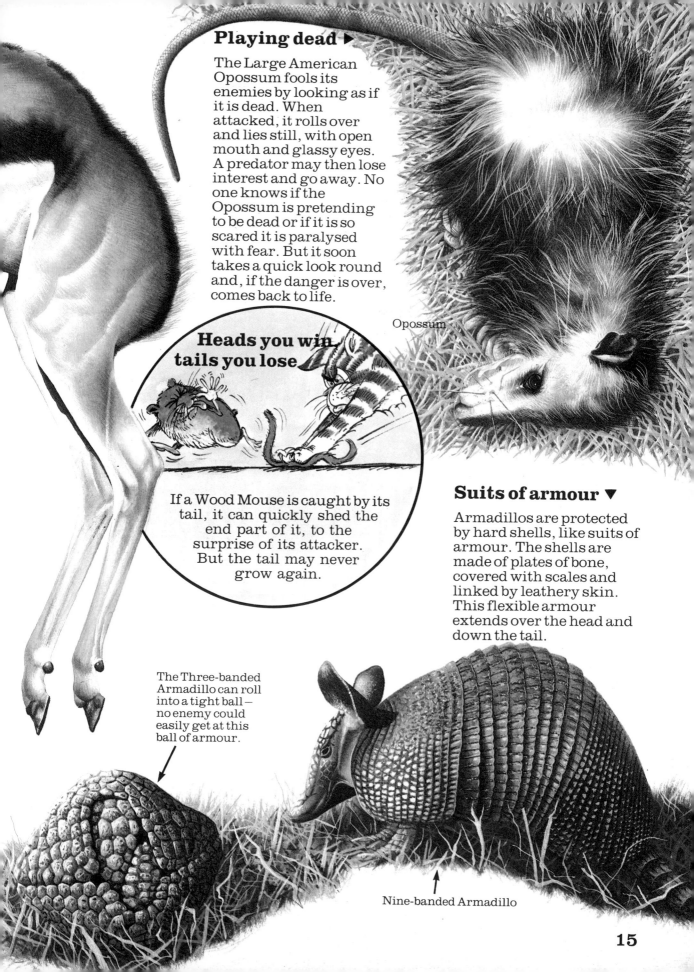

15

Attack, fight or bluff?

The horns grow longer each year, adding a new ridge and curling round at the tips.

Bighorn rams

Fighting rams ▲

These Bighorn rams clash heads in a fight for the females of the herd at the start of the mating season. Often one ram will give in to another with larger horns but two rams of equal size may end with bruised heads. For the rest of the year, rams live peacefully in a herd separate from the females.

Massive horns

An African Buffalo bull can fight off an attack by a lioness with slashing sweeps of its horns. It also charges other buffalo bulls during the mating season but the smaller, younger ones usually give in without injury.

The antlers, which are made of bone, begin to grow again each spring.

A bull Moose has the biggest horns of all deer.

◀ Annual display

The bull Moose grows a new, larger set of antlers each year, adding two more points until they are up to 2 metres wide. At the end of the summer, the covering of soft, furry skin, called velvet, begins to drop off. The bull then cleans and polishes his antlers before challenging other bulls to duels to win females of the herd. When mating is over, the antlers fall off.

Rubbing off the itching velvet to polish the antlers.

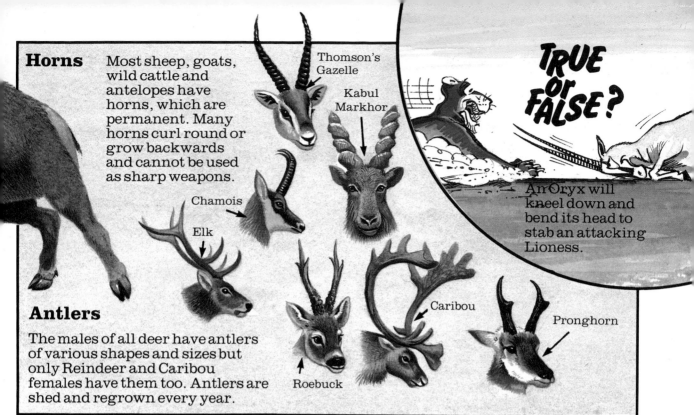

Horns

Most sheep, goats, wild cattle and antelopes have horns, which are permanent. Many horns curl round or grow backwards and cannot be used as sharp weapons.

Thomson's Gazelle

Kabul Markhor

Chamois

Elk

Antlers

The males of all deer have antlers of various shapes and sizes but only Reindeer and Caribou females have them too. Antlers are shed and regrown every year.

Roebuck

Caribou

Pronghorn

TRUE or FALSE?

An Oryx will kneel down and bend its head to stab an attacking Lioness.

Threatening tusks ▼

The Hippopotamus has huge teeth but it only feeds on plants, tearing them off with its rubbery lips. A female Hippo may use her teeth to defend her calf against a hungry crocodile. And a bull, fighting to establish his territory against other bulls, may cause terrible wounds with his teeth.

Hippopotamus

A Hippo's yawn is a threat to other bulls and may start a fight.

Sharp fangs ▼

A Lioness uses her long, sharp fangs to kill her prey with one deep bite. Her other teeth act like shears for cutting meat and grinding it up. Several Lionesses hunt together, stalking and ambushing food for the pride.

Strong jaws for holding on to prey.

Lioness

Deep freeze mammals

Snowshoes ▶

The Snowshoe Hare gets its name from its huge hind feet which act like snowshoes when it runs and leaps across soft snow. Long hair grows between the toes and the side of the feet, keeping them warm and giving a grip on frozen snow. The Hare is white during the North American winter but turns brown in spring.

In winter the Hare feeds on twigs and bark, or scrapes away the snow to find roots.

The huge footprints leave little scent for predators to follow.

The Beaver's "lodge" has a room above the water and underwater entrances.

Lodge built of branches and mud.

Macaques groom each other when sitting in hot pools.

Japanese Macaques

Beaver dragging felled branch to underwater foodstore.

Food in the freezer

Beavers collect branches in the autumn and store them in a pile next to their "lodge". During the winter they feed on the bark, reaching the store through an underwater tunnel when the lake is frozen over. Each family has its own lodge. It can be so warm inside that steam sometimes rises from its ventilation hole in very cold weather.

Making hay while the sun shines ▼

A Pika makes a short piercing whistle as it works at "haymaking".

The supply of food has to last for over four months during the winter.

The Pika makes hay during the summer to eat in the winter when the ground is covered with snow. It collects grass and herbs, spreads them out in the sun to dry and then carries them to a "haystack" in a rocky crevice. Each Pika builds its own haystacks, guarding them fiercely against the rest of the colony.

Food under the snow ▶

When snow covers the ground, Reindeer scrape holes in it to eat the "moss" underneath. No one knows how they find the plant, which is really a lichen, but they may be able to smell it.

It needs 12 kilos of spongy green lichen a day in winter.

The Reindeer has broad, splayed hoofs for walking on snow and soft ground.

TRUE or FALSE?

When hunting seals, Polar Bears cover up their black noses with a paw.

◀ Long hot baths

Macaques in northern Japan keep warm in winter by taking baths in hot volcanic springs. They come out, wet and dripping, to search for meals of seeds and bark.

Living with heat and drought

A Kangaroo Rat hops about the desert collecting seeds, pushing them into its cheek pouches with its front paws.

Leaps over 2 metres up into the air to escape predators.

◀ Desert drought

Kangaroo Rats can survive without water by living on dried seeds. They make their own fluids from these seeds and keep cool during the heat of the day by sealing themselves up in underground burrows. This preserves the moisture they breathe out. They also eat their own droppings for the moisture and vitamins they contain.

Mud bather

After feeding in the early morning, Rhinos wallow in mud holes, swamps or lakes in the heat of the afternoon. A cooling bath lowers the body temperature and protects a Rhinoceros from biting insects which get into the folds and wrinkles of its thick skin.

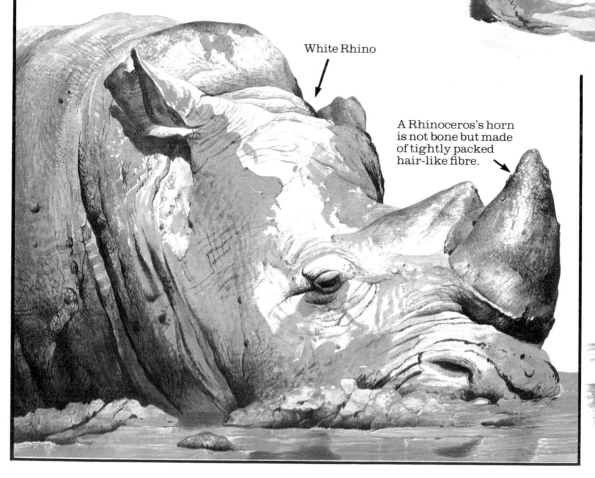

White Rhino

A Rhinoceros's horn is not bone but made of tightly packed hair-like fibre.

A cooling dip ▼

Tigers do not like very hot weather and spend the day lying in long grass or taking a cooling dip in shallow water. They are strong swimmers and will catch fish and turtles when food is scarce.

A solitary hunter, a tiger silently stalks its prey. When close enough it pounces, holding on and biting until the animal is dead.

Giant ears

The Antelope Jack Rabbit's huge ears help it to keep cool as it rests in the shade during the day. Arteries carry hot blood to the ears where the heat disperses into the air. The Rabbit, which is really a desert hare, faces north to catch the slightly cooler air.

Antelope Jack Rabbits can run as fast as 56 kph to escape from predators.

Ears up to 20 centimetres long held up to catch cool air.

TRUE or FALSE?

Camels store water in their humps during a drought in the desert.

Sleeping it off ▶

The Mojave Squirrel lives through long winter droughts by sleeping for up to five days a week in its burrow. Protected from the desert heat, it saves energy and needs little food.

Eats any desert plants including cacti.

Mojave Squirrel

Burrow 1 metre underground linked by 3 metre tunnels.

Digs burrow in August.

Clever co-ordinators

Defending the young ▼

Musk oxen live in small herds in the Arctic tundra. When attacked by wolves, the adults form a defensive wall to protect the calves. A male ox steps forward to do battle. If he falls, others follow, one by one, until the attack is repelled.

African Oxpeckers on a Warthog's back may warn it of danger by retreating to the far side of the animal and making noisy calls.

Musk oxen's shaggy coats have two layers, a long coarse outer with a fine wool one underneath.

Chimpanzees comb through each other's coarse black hair with hands that are good at grasping as well as picking out tiny seeds, dirt and lice.

They travel and rest on the ground but feed and sleep in the trees.

Friendly groomers

Chimpanzees spend many hours a day grooming each other. This keeps their fur clean and also helps to keep them together in a friendly group. Grooming is such a pleasure that chimpanzees sometimes sit in chains, stroking and picking at each other's fur. But during these times of rest, they must always be alert for prowling leopards and other predators.

Oxpecker

Warthog

Ants under the scales

The Pangolin eats ants but it also uses them as cleaners. It raises its scales to let the ants crawl underneath. They eat the parasites that the Pangolin cannot scratch off itself.

There are stories that the Pangolin will then go off to the nearest pool. When it is underwater, it opens its scales so that the ants float out and it licks them up with its tongue.

The Pangolin has sharp overlapping scales. When curled in a ball it is safe from any attack.

Insect-pecking birds ▲

Oxpecker birds spend most of their day perched on large animals, such as Giraffes, Antelopes or Warthogs, busily pecking at ticks and biting flies. The animal ignores them unless they peck too painfully in ears, round eyes or at wounds.

TRUE or FALSE?

Do rats help each other to move eggs which are too large for one rat to carry?

Honey Guide Bird

Honey Badger

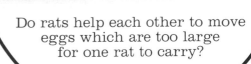

A Honey Badger's thick, loose coat is good protection against bee and wasp stings.

Wild bees' nest

◀ The nest robbers

The Honey Guide Bird works with the Honey Badger to find their favourite foods. The Bird flits from tree to tree, calling noisily, to lead the Badger to a bees' nest. The Badger claws it open and they feast together — the Badger on honey and grubs, the Bird on beeswax.

23

Communicating

The Indri lives in the forests of Madagascar.

Colourful heads and tails

A male Mandrill bares his teeth to show that he submits to an older male.

The male Mandrill's brilliantly coloured face, and bottom of the same colours, warn other males to keep away from his family group.

Wailing Indri ▲

The Indri has a very loud, wailing call. A family group often wails in concert for several minutes. This seems to alert straying members of the group and warns other groups to keep their distance.

Kissing friends ▼

Prairie dogs "kiss" when they meet to find out if they are from the same group. If they are, they groom each other. If not, they fight and the intruder is driven away. Prairie dogs live in huge underground burrows or "towns" containing hundreds, even thousands, of animals. Each family group has its own section which it defends against strangers.

TRUE or FALSE?

Lonely Wolves howl at the moon.

Prairie Dogs

Sentries keep watch at the entrance to Prairie Dog burrows, barking a warning at the first sign of danger.

Booming pouches ▼

A male Orang Utan calls and "burps" to tell other males to keep out of his territory. He fills his throat pouch with air, swelling his face, and lets out a long call, ending with bubbling burps and sighs.

The heaviest of all the tree-dwellers, male Orang Utans may be over 1½ metres tall and weigh 200 kilos.

Old male Orang Utans have huge cheeks which are stores of fat for times when fruit is scarce.

Scent signals

The Ring-tailed Lemur rubs its bottom on trees as it goes through the forest, leaving its scent to mark its trail for the rest of the troop.

Before the annual mating season, males have "stink fights" for females. A male rubs his wrists against scent glands near his armpits, brings his tail between his legs and rubs scent all over it. Then he faces his rival, fanning the scent forwards with his bristling tail. These battles also take place when two troops meet at the edges of their territories.

A Ring-tailed Lemur spends most of the time on the forest floor. It keeps its tail up to show the rest of the troop where it is.

Living in family groups of about 20, they sleep in the trees, moving on each morning in search of fruit to eat.

Mysterious behaviour

◀ Give and take rats

The Trade Rat, or Pack Rat, gets its name from its curious habit of stealing a bright, shiny object during the night and leaving a small stone or twig in its place. It stores these in its large untidy nest. There are stories of stolen jewellery, spectacles and even of a Trade Rat carrying away a burning candle.

Brown Hare

The swimming monkey ▼

Proboscis Monkey

This male monkey's huge nose probably boosts the sound of its honks as it calls through the mangrove swamps of Borneo. The female's nose is much smaller. Good swimmers, they jump into the water to search for mangrove shoots on which they feed.

In 1950, a Proboscis Monkey was seen swimming in the China sea, far out from the Borneo coast. A lifeboat was lowered from a cruise ship and the exhausted monkey climbed aboard. After resting for a while, it dived back into the sea and swam away. No one knows where it was going or if it reached dry land.

Alert ears catch the slightest sound of danger.

Strong hind legs for leaps of up to 5 metres.

Mad March boxers

In Spring, Hares have boxing matches and wild acrobatic games, which gave them their name of Mad March Hares. For years, no one really knew why they behaved like this. The latest theory is that it is part of their courtship ritual. Before mating, males and females — it is very difficult to tell them apart at a distance — chase each other. A female may also punch a male on the nose and tear fur from his back with her teeth if he tries to mate with her before she is ready.

Chimpanzees

Dancing chimps

At the beginning of a heavy storm male chimpanzees have been seen performing amazing rain dances. They stamp their feet, sway from side to side, tear the branches off trees and may race wildly up and down slopes in the forest. Watched by females and young chimpanzees sitting in the trees, these wild dances can last for 15 minutes or more.

Apple thieves

A Hedgehog carrying apples is an unusual sight. Reports say that a hedgehog collects a pile of apples and rolls on them so that some stick to its spines. It then takes them back to its nest in a hollow wall or empty rabbit burrow.

Mass migrations ▶

Every three or four years lemmings suddenly set off on mass migrations. Thousands swarm down the mountains of Norway and try to swim across rivers and even the sea. So many drown that it was thought they were on a suicide trek. It is now known that when food is plentiful, lemmings breed at a fantastic rate. As the population grows, food and places to live become scarce. Then the lemmings migrate in search of food and new homes.

Fact or fiction?

Mysterious monster ▼

Many people claim to have seen a monster in Loch Ness, Scotland. Underwater cameras and sonar have produced no proof but it has been suggested the monster is really a line of otters or a herd of swimming elephants.

Trunk of elephant swimming in Loch Ness?

Gazelle boy ▼

In a desert in the Middle East, a boy was spotted running with a herd of gazelles. He was later captured and adopted by a foster-mother. She said he behaved and ate like a gazelle, he refused the food she gave him and wanted to eat grass. She believed he had been brought up from a baby with the gazelles.

A boy was found living with a herd of gazelles.

Ape man's hands

In China an ape-man was said to have been killed after it attacked a small girl in 1957. Its hands were preserved and hair, a nest and footprints were also found in the area.

The ape-man's palms were 14 cm long.

The long-armed creature, it is said, stands upright except when climbing up steep ground.

Huge footprints ▶

There have been many reports of wild men – half human, half ape – from the remote parts of the world. They come from the Soviet Union, the United States, India and China. Usually only huge footprints are seen in snow or mud and these are quite different from the prints of any large animal, such as a bear. People living in the Himalayas say they have seen the Yeti, a tall shambling figure which stands upright and makes high-pitched calls.

Footprints of a Yeti in hard snow were 80 cms long and 40 cms wide.

Animal showers ▶

Do animals fall from the sky? On the Indonesian island of Lambok, the people said that in 1968 rats fell on to their rice fields. The rats came down in bunches of seven, led by a huge white rat. There have also been stories of showers of frogs, fish, snails, lizards and rattlesnakes.

A shower of rats falling on rice fields on an Indonesian island.

Wolf children ▼

Many stories have been told of children brought up by wolves. The most famous is of two Indian girls, aged about seven and two years old, who were found in 1920 romping with a pack of wolves. They crawled about, eating only meat and howling. Taken to an orphanage, the eldest learned to stand up and say a few words but died when she was about 17.

Indian girls grew up with a pack of wolves.

Ape man

This strange creature, which had been shot through the head, was kept in a block of ice by a showman in the United States. He would not say where it came from or how he got hold of it in 1968. A Belgium zoologist, who examined it through the cloudy ice, was sure it was not a fake. This ape-man was 2 metres tall with long arms and huge hands. In many ways it was like the short, stocky Neanderthal Man, an ancestor of human beings, who was thought to have lived about 50,000 years ago.

Record breakers

Highest jumper

Both Pumas and African Leopards have been seen to jump 5½ metres up into a tree. A hunted kangaroo leapt over a pile of timber 3 metres high.

Fastest mammal

The Cheetah has been timed at 110 kph over short distances. Over longer distances, a Pronghorn Antelope clocked 67 kph for 1.6 km, and one was reportedly timed at 98 kph for 183 metres. A race horse runs at about 70 kph.

Largest land animal

The largest land animal is the male African Elephant. The largest recorded was 3.8 metres high at the shoulder, 10 metres from the tip of its tail to the end of its trunk, and weighed about 10.8 tonnes.

Slowest mammal

The Three-toed Sloth moves along the ground at a speed of about 2 metres a minute. Through the trees, it is a little faster – about 3 metres per minute. Answering a distress call from her baby, a mother sloth was seen to "sprint" 4 metres in a minute.

Smallest land mammal

From head to tail adult Etruscan Shrews measure between 6 and 8 cms – the tails are about 2.5 cms long – and weigh 1.5-2.5 grams.

Tallest animal

Bull Giraffes are usually 5 metres tall although there are reports of 7 metre ones being shot. The tallest recorded bull lived at Chester Zoo, England, and grew to 6 metres.

Man-eating cats

A Tigress in Nepal and Kumaon killed 437 people in eight years, before being shot in 1911. A Leopard in Panar, India, accounted for over 400 victims.

Largest litter

The Common Tenrec, which is found mainly in Madagascar, gives birth to litters of 32 or 33 babies.

Oldest animal

The Asiatic Elephant can live to be 70 years old and may survive to be 80.

Longest horn

The longest front horn on a White Rhinoceros measured 158 cm. Explorers' reports of a beast with a horn may had led to the myth of the unicorn.

Most dangerous bat

The Vampire Bat of tropical America can transmit a number of diseases when it sucks blood. In Latin America 1 million cattle die every year from rabies passed on by this bat and there are a number of human deaths too.

Largest wingspan

The Kalong, a fruit bat of Malaysia, has a wingspan of 170 cms.

Largest herd

In the 19th century, vast herds of Springbok, numbering perhaps 100 million, migrated in search of food. One herd was said to be 24 kilometres wide and more than 150 kilometres long.

Longest tusks

The right tusk of the longest pair of elephant tusks measured 3.48 metres along its outside curve. Together the tusks weighed 117 kilograms.

Smallest flying mammal

Thailand's Bumblebee Bat has a wingspan of 160 mm, a length of 29-33 mm and weighs about 2 grams.

Longest pregnancy

The Asiatic Elephant usually carries its young for about 20 months but pregnancies can last for over 2 years before the single calf is born.

Rarest animal

The rarest animal, which may already be extinct, is the Thylacine, or Tasmanian Wolf. It has not been positively seen for over 50 years and has probably never been photographed in the wild.

Highest living

The Yak sometimes climbs up to an altitude of 6,100 feet in the Himalayas.

Were they true or false?

Page 5 When a Hippo mother goes off to feed, she finds a babysitter.
True. Each group of Hippos has a central nursery where the females and young gather. If a mother goes out of it, she leaves her calf with another female.

Page 7 Goats in Tunisia jump on donkeys' backs to reach leaves on high branches of trees.
Maybe. There are reports that the goats have been seen butting the donkeys into position under the trees but they have never been photographed.

Page 8 The Gibbon is a tightrope artist.
True. The Gibbon will walk upright on its hind legs along tree-top vines. Other monkeys use legs and arms to walk along vines.

Page 11 Frog-eating Bats choose the juiciest frog by listening to its mating call.
True and false. These Bats can tell edible frogs from the poisonous ones by the mating calls, but cannot tell which ones will make the biggest meal.

Page 12 The Black Panther really does exist.
True, but it is just a black form of the Leopard.

Page 14 A Porcupine can shoot its quills at an enemy.
False, but if an enemy touches the quills, they come loose and stick in its skin.

Page 17 An Oryx will kneel down and bend its head to stab an attacking Lioness.
True. Instead of running away, an Oryx will sometimes bravely face a Lioness. When kneeling down with bent head, its backward-sloping horns point forwards and can cause serious injuries.

Page 19 When hunting seals, Polar Bears cover up their black noses.
Probably false, although one scientist claimed that a Polar Bear sometimes covers its nose so that it does not show up against its white fur and the snow.

Page 21 Camels store water in their humps during a drought in the desert.
False. Their humps are lumps of fat which they live on when food is scarce.

Page 23 Rats help each other to move eggs which are too large for one rat to carry.
Maybe. There have been reports that Rats move eggs by forming chains and passing the egg along, or one Rat drags another holding an egg. But there is no real scientific proof.

Page 24 Lonely Wolves howl at the moon.
False. Wolves do howl at night but this is to keep in touch with the rest of the pack and to warn other packs away from their territory.

Index